THE PARTY

THE PARTY

By David McPhail

Hooked On Phonics®

To Kolya and Andreas
and their father,
Brother Jack

First published in 1990 by Little, Brown and Company.
This edition published in 1998 by Gateway Learning Corporation.
Copyright © 1998 Gateway Learning Corporation. All rights reserved.
Printed in China. No part of this publication may be reproduced, stored in any
retrieval system or transmitted, in any form or by any means, electronic, mechanical,
photocopying, recording, or otherwise, without the prior written permission of the publisher.
ISBN 1-887942-51-3   6 7 8 9 10

It is nighttime.
We are planning a party—
my animal pals and I.

The party is just about to begin
when my dad comes in to read us a story.

But just at the best part . . .

he goes to sleep.

"We can't have a party now!" says Bear.

"We will have to wake him up," I say.

We push and we poke, but my dad does not even stir.

We try tickling him,
but my dad keeps right on sleeping.

"We'll have a party anyway!" I tell my pals.

And we do.
We blow up balloons.
The ones that Bear blows up are so full of hot air
that we can hang onto them and float!

When we are over the bed we let go . . .
and BOUNCE!

After that we take a ride on my electric train.

"Duck, everybody!" I yell.

"We are going through a tunnel!"

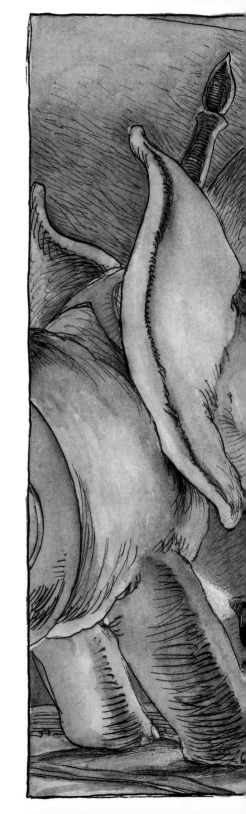

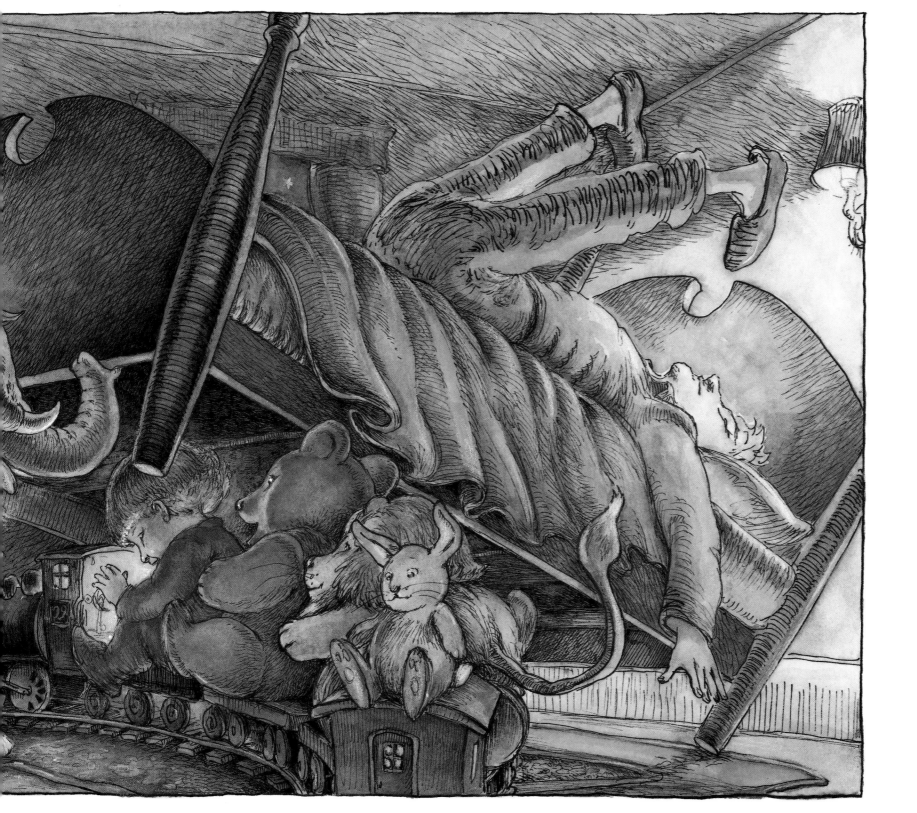

13

We make music and dance.
Bear is getting hungry.
"What's a party without food?" he asks.

So we go down to the kitchen
for something to eat.

My dad comes, too.

In the kitchen we help ourselves
to all the food we can find.

I make sandwiches for everybody.

While we are eating, I hear my mom call my dad.
"Are you coming to bed, dear?" she asks.
"Quick!" I say. "We have got to get back upstairs!"

It is not easy.

But we finally make it.

We stand my dad up and give him a little push.

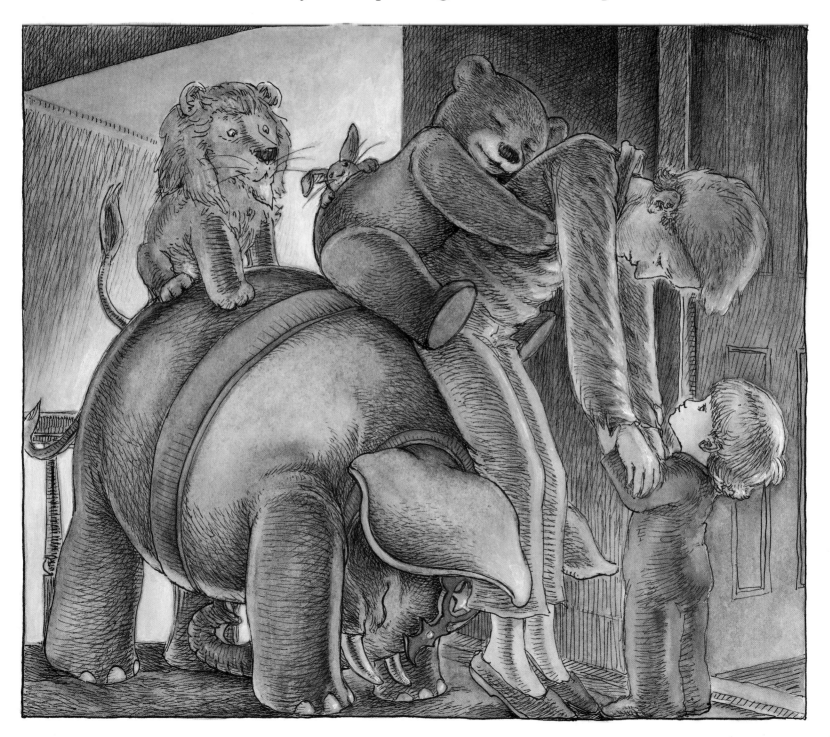

"Good night, Dad," I whisper.

"There you are, dear," says my mom. "Were you having a snack?"

We quietly close the door.
"What shall we do now?" I ask.
"Well," says Bear, "I'm still hungry. . . ."

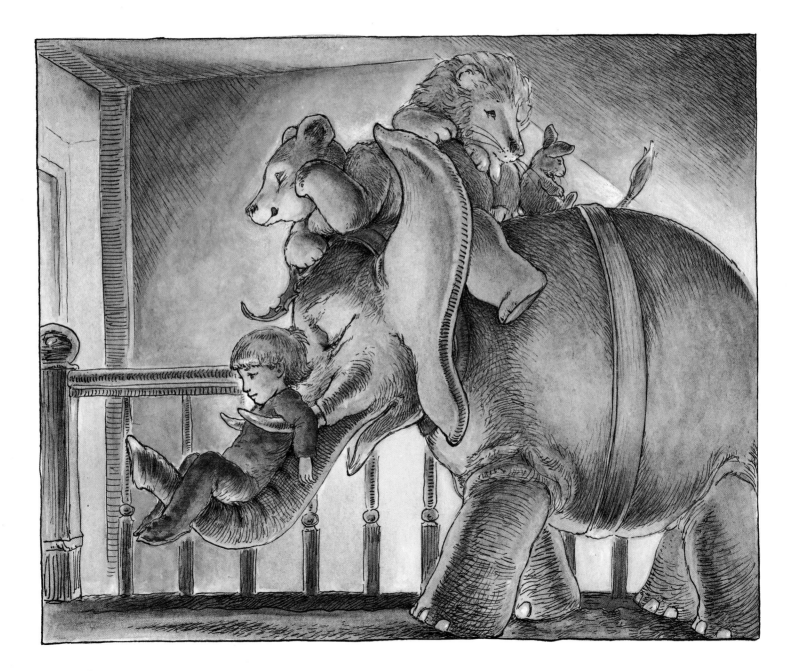